D1416559

A Note to Parents and Caregivers:

Read-it! Readers are for children who are just starting on the amazing road to reading. These beautiful books support both the acquisition of reading skills and the love of books.

The PURPLE LEVEL presents basic topics and objects using high frequency words and simple language patterns.

The RED LEVEL presents familiar topics using common words and repeating sentence patterns.

The BLUE LEVEL presents new ideas using a larger vocabulary and varied sentence structure.

The YELLOW LEVEL presents more challenging ideas, a broad vocabulary, and wide variety in sentence structure.

The GREEN LEVEL presents more complex ideas, an extended vocabulary range, and expanded language structures.

The ORANGE LEVEL presents a wide range of ideas and concepts using challenging vocabulary and complex language structures.

When sharing a book with your child, read in short stretches, pausing often to talk about the pictures. Have your child turn the pages and point to the pictures and familiar words. And be sure to reread favorite stories or parts of stories.

There is no right or wrong way to share books with children. Find time to read with your child, and pass on the legacy of literacy.

Adria F. Klein, Ph.D.
Professor Emeritus
California State University
San Bernardino, California

Editor: Christianne Jones
Designer: Joe Anderson
Page Production: Tracy Kaehler
Creative Director: Keith Griffin
Editorial Director: Carol Jones
The illustrations in this book were created with acrylic paints.

Picture Window Books
5115 Excelsior Boulevard
Suite 232
Minneapolis, MN 55416
877-845-8392
www.picturewindowbooks.com

Printed in the United States of America.

Library of Congress Cataloging-in-Publication Data
Dougherty, Terri.
The bath / by Terri Dougherty ; illustrated by Hye Won Yi.
p. cm. — (Read-it! readers)
Summary: After planting flowers in the yard, Tanya and her dog Rudy both need a
bath, but who will get to use the soap first?
ISBN 1-4048-1576-7 (hardcover)
[1. Baths—Fiction. 2. Dogs—Fiction. 3. Brothers and sisters—Fiction.] I. Yi, Hye
Won, 1979- ill. II. Title. III. Series.

PZ7.D74436Bat 2005
[E]—dc22   2005021440

The Bath

by Terri Dougherty
illustrated by Hye Won Yi

Special thanks to our advisers for their expertise:

Adria F. Klein, Ph.D.
Professor Emeritus, California State University
San Bernardino, California

Susan Kesselring, M.A.
Literacy Educator
Rosemount–Apple Valley–Eagan (Minnesota) School District

PICTURE WINDOW BOOKS
Minneapolis, Minnesota

"It's a great day to plant flowers,"
Tanya said.

Tanya and her dog, Rudy, raced into the backyard.

Tanya dug holes for marigolds and petunias.

Rudy dug holes for himself.

Tanya planted flower after flower.

Rudy dug hole after hole.

The yard was beautiful, but Tanya was not. "I need a bath," she said.

"So does Rudy," her brother
Raymond said.

"I need soap, a washcloth, and a towel," Tanya said.

She went inside to get her bath stuff.

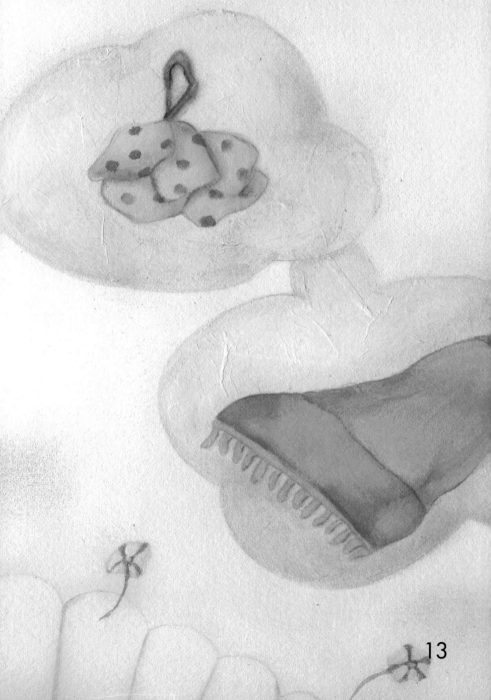

The soap was not in the soap dish.

The washcloth was not by the sink.

The towel was not on the rack.

Tanya looked out the window.
Raymond was carrying the
soap, the washcloth, and
the towel.

"Raymond!" Tanya yelled out the window.

"Why did you take all of my bath stuff? I need it for my bath!"

"I need the soap, the washcloth, and the towel, too," Raymond said.

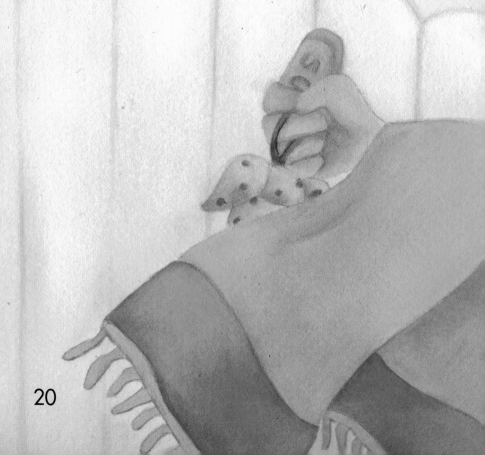

"Rudy needs a bath!"

Tanya went into the backyard. Raymond was filling a little swimming pool with water and soap.

"Jump in!" he said to Tanya and Rudy.

Tanya jumped in. Rudy jumped in with her. A mountain of bubbles grew as they splashed and scrubbed.

Soon, Tanya and Rudy were clean.

27

But now someone else was dirty.

"Raymond, you need a bath!"
Tanya said.

31

More *Read-it!* Readers

Bright pictures and fun stories help you practice your reading skills. Look for more books at your level.

Back to School 1-4048-1166-4
The Best Snowman 1-4048-0048-4
Bill's Baggy Pants 1-4048-0050-6
Camping Trip 1-4048-1167-2
Days of the Week 1-4048-1581-3
Eric Won't Do It 1-4048-1188-5
Fable's Whistle 1-4048-1169-9
Finny Learns to Swim 1-4048-1582-1
Goldie's New Home 1-4048-1171-0
I Am in Charge of Me 1-4048-0646-6
The Lazy Scarecrow 1-4048-0062-X
Little Joe's Big Race 1-4048-0063-8
The Little Star 1-4048-0065-4
Meg Takes a Walk 1-4048-1005-6
The Naughty Puppy 1-4048-0067-0
Paula's Letter 1-4048-1183-4
Riley Flies a Kite 1-4048-1586-4
Selfish Sophie 1-4048-0069-7
The Tall, Tall Slide 1-4048-1186-9
The Traveling Shoes 1-4048-1588-0
A Trip to the Zoo 1-4048-1590-2
Willy the Worm 1-4048-1593-7

Looking for a specific title or level? A complete list of *Read-it!* Readers is available on our Web site:
www.picturewindowbooks.com